Emilio

Social Rejects Syndicate

An Andino Crime Family Novel

USA Today Bestselling Author

Eden Rose

<u>EMILO</u>

This book is a work of fiction. The names, characters, places, and incidents are all products of the author's imagination and are not to be construed as real. Any resemblances to persons, organizations, events, or locales are entirely coincidental.

Cover design by Sweet 15 Designs

Publishing by Pink Ribbon Publishing

Emilo

Social Rejects Syndicate

An Andino Crime Family Novel

USA Today Bestselling Author

Eden Rose

Prologue

Larysa

Quickly, I adjust my strapless dress as I await the trap door to open up above me. The platform I'm standing on is hard and my heels slide on the tile while hyping myself up.

This marks my fourth show in four days and I'm tired. I love the touring season mainly because of the traveling, but I get tired after three shows in a row. Plus, I miss my home.

The telltale sign of the trap door springing open and the creak of the platform beneath me has me ready to end this show strong.

My managers wanted me to do so many shows in such a short amount of time to build the energy and excitement of my new album. Also, this is the only show I have done since I broke up with Arnoldo after rumors of him cheating on me started to surface.

"Larysa! Larysa!"

"Hello!" I holler out to my fans as I fly through the trap door. All I can see is the shape of the bodies in the audience with the lights flashing in my eyes of my light show. I love seeing the faces of my fans because it lets me know I'm actually doing all of this for a reason. Of course, the money is good.

But the money isn't going to keep me warm at night.

"Larysa! Larysa!" The crowd screams again with more energy than before.

I smile at everyone. My band is behind me ready to begin my next song in my act. The dancers get into position around me and I smile at them.

"All right. Should we do an old favorite?" I ask my fans.

The screams from the audience tell me I should.

After two songs, I'm finally finished with my show. I'm ready to take these heels off and throw myself into the car to go back to the hotel room. I'm needing to relax for a couple of days.

"Thank you everyone for being here! I truly love you all and can't thank you enough for being here," I croon out while bowing two more times.

I'm walking off the stage when Alto, my security guard who is with me at all times, is rushing me through the back hallways. I'm trying to dig my heels into the ground to get him to stop, but it doesn't work. Whatever he is sensing that is happening must be serious.

"Alto!" I scream out as he picks me up and holds me close to his chest.

He doesn't say anything until we're seated in the limo with me tucked in the middle. I'm about to start demanding why he's acting like this when I see a bright flashing light off to the side.

My stalker has followed me here.

"When did you find out he was here?" I ask quietly. I'm secretly not ready for the answer.

My stalker has been following me for over a year and each time he shows up, he leaves just in the nick of time so we can't do anything. He is an average-looking guy with nothing too extreme besides his crazy-looking eyes.

"Stop talking," Alto mutters in Greek.

The high from my show dissipates as we pull up to my favorite hotel and resort on Mount Olympus. I have loved this place since I was a little girl and my father took me here to go skiing. Skiing used to be one of my favorite past times before the craziness of being a pop star kicked in.

Alto bangs on the door twice to get the driver's attention and then nods towards me. I have always known that to mean he wants the driver to drive around back without too much flare.

He's worried the stalker will follow us here and doesn't want too much of an audience.

I have seen the damage Alto can do to someone and it isn't pretty. I once watched Alto stab someone in the stomach with a knife that expands inside the human body. It was horrifying to watch, but the person was trying to come on to me.

Alto will do anything to protect me.

People are surrounding the limo with Alto is guiding me out of the limo and pulling me through the entrance of the lodge. I'm walking as calmly as I can with his hand gripping my elbow. Someone jumps out at me from the corner and I scream.

My bodyguard has my head to his chest and his arm is wrapped around my back to hold me snuggly against him. I feel him push people out of the way until we are in the ski lodge.

Once we are in the lodge, Alto doesn't stop until we are on the elevator. I lightly push out of his hold to look around the elevator. The last time I came here, there wasn't a second-floor back then.

I see glass shards, flowers spread all over the entryway to my room at the ski lodge along with pictures of me photoshopped on dead bodies. My mouth drops to the ground.

"Why is this happening?" I mutter to Alto. "Why can't he leave me alone?"

Chapter One

Emilio

It isn't very often that Octavious calls for sit-downs with outsiders. It also isn't very often that he looks so uncomfortable with this outsider in our meeting space.

"You mean to tell me, you want to hire one of my guys to follow around some spoiled popstar?" Octavious asks with his mouth agape.

One thing Octavious doesn't like to do is deal with stupid shit like this. Since when are we bodyguards to some popstar princess? This is the dumbest shit I have ever heard. If we're getting hired to do something, it is taking someone out... Not keeping them alive.

The man standing in front of us looks pissed that he's asking for help. He looks as if it is physically painful for him to be standing in a room full of Andino Family members.

"I wouldn't be here if I didn't have another option. Larysa is being targeted by some creep who wants her dead. He's been following her for the past year and won't give her up."

I've seen music videos of Larysa and she's sexy for being a pop star. I'm not into the whole high-maintenance bull shit, but she's not bad-looking. Granted her music isn't the best, she's got a good voice.

Octavious nods and looks over at me. Protection is something I've done my whole life. Octavious recruited me from working at a couple of bars as a bouncer to start doing side jobs for him. I loved the quick cash I would get with the Andinos and quickly jumped over to this side.

I shake my head at him to indicate that I'm not interested. The last thing I want to do is follow around Larysa while she's touring Europe or whatever. Plus, the family needs me here. The family needs me here to make sure things are running smoothly. With Octavious and Milo all wifed up, it is only a matter of time before one of their chicks becomes knocked up and then they will need the extra security.

"Why can't you do it?" I blurt with a snarl. I'm sitting next to Milo and Miklos around the table drinking out of my Scotch tumbler. There is something about drinking a two-fingered Scotch that has me almost considering the job.

It has been a long time since I've been with someone outside of this realm. It would be nice to be with someone new.

What the fuck am I thinking? I'm actually considering this?

The man in front shifts his weight on his feet. This is a clear indicator he's nervous and doesn't want to be here anymore than we want him here.

"I've been with Larysa for a long time and have fought off a lot of these fuckers. This guy is different. This guy broke into your ski lodge and vandalized her room. Broke your glass mirrors…" He takes a breath before continuing. "I wouldn't be here if I wasn't worried about her. You know what happened to Elena," he mutters.

Elena was a Spanish pop star which everyone loved. Her music played over the radio so much your eyes would roll when you would hear it play. The woman was gorgeous, sexy and a talented singer and everyone loved her. Unfortunately, one of her fans broke into her home in Spain and set the whole house on fire with Elena and the fan inside. It was tragic and easily avoidable if her bodyguard would have picked up on the signs.

"What is the stalker doing?" I question. I need to know exactly what I'm getting into before I start this bull shit. I don't want to be caught up in the middle of it.

The man nods towards me and reaches around to his back pocket. The way he does it is too quick making all of us pull out our guns and aim them at him. He chuckles. "I'm getting my phone. Jesus Christ."

He pulls out his phone and types in a security code. Soon enough, he's thrusting it into my face for me to see all of the pictures that were taken of Larysa and what has happened to her stuff.

Sure enough, there are doors broke into, there are notes with cut-out magazine lettering… There is a lot of the typical shit stalkers do. The one thing that I see that has me clutching the phone is a security camera aimed at her room and seeing someone sneaking into the room to jerk off.

"You haven't gotten close enough to him?"

The man shrugs. "I've not been able to get him. I need a second pair of eyes and muscle to ensure he doesn't get her. I'm Alto, Larysa's lead security detail."

"Emilio," I mutter almost inaudibly. "What do you say, boss?" I ask Octavious.

"How much is the job paying?"

Alto clears his throat. "There are a couple of things I need to say first before we talk money. I need to make sure you're not going to tell her about her room. That will freak her out."

I shrug him off. I don't need him telling me what to do and what not to do. If I'm protecting her, I will do whatever the fuck I want.

"And I need you to take point from me."

That statement, I have to laugh. "You're asking us for help. Why would I let you take point?" I huff out.

The guys burst out laughing, too. They know I'm not the type to take orders from other people.

He shifts again on his feet. "I know this girl. She's going to flip out if she finds out what's been going on when she's not paying attention."

"How much?" Octavious asks.

"Twenty-five large a week to keep her safe. I'm thinking I'll need you for about a week or two."

I down my drink and then consider the option. It's a fair amount of money but I want double. "Make it double and we're good."

Chapter Two

Larysa

Looking at the aftermath of my last show scattered and trashed in my room, I feel the sinking feeling overtake me. I have never kept my anxiety and depression from my fans or any of the team. I've been open about it and I like to keep it that way.

At first, I wanted to hide my mental health status from my fans and team. It took me quite a bit of courage to be open with people about my anxiety coupled with depression and then I finally opened up. It felt a lot more real when I told my fans who poured so much love out for me. It was amazing.

These pictures of me doing everyday stuff is what has me drowning in anxiety. Every ounce of self-coping skills I have developed has flown out the window. This asshole has pictures of me using the bathroom, getting out of the shower, eating dinner, walking my dog and putting on makeup. Everything I do during the day has been photographed.

I'm walking around the carnage with my hands on my head trying to wrap my brain on why I'm being targeted. My silk robe swishes around my legs giving me a sense of touch. I look at the pictures of me sleeping and this is the one that has me screaming.

Alto is rushing through the door with a random man following behind him. I don't have a spare moment to question why this man is following behind him because Alto is pulling me into his chest.

"What's wrong, kitten?" Alto mutters against my ear.

The affectionate nickname Alto has called me ever since he met me has me calming a little. Alto is great at what he does and I'm only assuming this stalker has him questioning how great he is.

If I were in a better place, I would tell him this wasn't his fault. It isn't anyone's fault besides the stalker's but I'm not. I'm wanting to blame my fear and frustrations out on someone, too. I don't want to direct it all at Alto, though. I know he's trying to protect me.

In the moments where my anxiety gets to be too much, it is hard to keep myself in check. It is hard to pay attention to the reality of what is going on.

Without saying a word, I point to the scattered pictures. The other man leans down and grabs the one of me self-pleasuring myself.

I'm mortified. I know everyone self-pleasures themselves, but I didn't need it to be photographed. Plus, I didn't need this random man to see me like that.

My ears turn red and I feel myself getting warm from the embarrassment. Alto rips the picture out of the man's hands and chucks it behind him.

"Uh, my name is Emilio," the sexy man mutters under his breath while looking me up and down. He's wearing a fitted Armani suit and making me remember my status of undress.

Looking at him, I consider what he's doing here. I'm running out of patience and decide to be rude and ask him anyway. "Who are you and why are you here?"

Alto clears his throat. "I've hired him to help me protect you."

I push out of his hold and begin to pace. My finger is caught mid-twirl in my hair which is one of my nervous habits I've picked up which pisses me off. I'm tired of people knowing so much about me and this is just another tell for them. "I have you. Why do I need someone else?"

"Larysa, this stalker is coming at you hard," he begins with his hands tucked in his suit pants. His body is quite large and intimidating for people who don't him. I know that he can fuck someone up big time and I try not to get him too mad at me. "I can't split myself in half until he's caught and I need someone to help. I wish I could, but I can't. This stalker isn't going to stop until you're dead."

I untangle my finger and look at the other guy. Emilio. "How could you protect me?" I'm asking a serious question. The last thing I need is someone more looking over my shoulder at everything I do. I don't need to feel like I'm being smothered.

Emilio's chocolate eyes light up. His lips are full and curved into a sinister smile that has my insides tightening. "Let's just say, I'm good at what I do. If you want to end up like the other popstar, not my fucking problem."

The bluntness of this man has me taken aback. Not many members of my team are as blunt and harsh as he just was. I must say, there is something sexy about the way he just told me that. My muscles are tightening on their own accord as my sexual frustration reminds me again how long it has been since I've had sex.

Alto grips my shoulders to stop my pacing. "The man brokc into your house in Greece and jacked off on your bed."

Hearing those words has me dropping to my knees to carrel all of the photos. Emilio gets down on his knees to place his hand over mine to stop me.

The electric shock wave that zings through my body is enough to make me want to scream. I'm so sexually frustrated, I'm considering jumping him. What kind of person does it make me to be turned on during a situation like this?

I'm fucked up. I need to go back to counseling.

"Let me help. If you're not satisfied," he stretches that word out, "I'll leave. I guarantee you will be satisfied, though. All of my customers are."

I'm not sure if he means to be as forward as he is sounding, but it sure sounds like that. I'm equally turned on, scared and something else I can't figure out.

Chapter Three

Emilio

Don't get me wrong, I've heard of Larysa before. Before today, she was just some random pop star I turn off the radio every time she comes on. I'm not interested in pop music and the bubble gum bull shit.

But this woman in front of me, she's sexy. Her eyes widen as my fingers trace her skin. Her eyes are watching mine and a slow smile curves those luscious lips of hers. She's turned on!

Alto clears his throat effectively ruining the moment we were sharing. "Are you ready to talk about her schedule?"

I'm zapped out of my hunter/prey mode and instantly back into business mode. I know I'm here for a reason and that's not fucking the shit out of this pretty woman in front of me. It isn't bending her over, lifting that silky robe off her ass and eating her out from behind either. Or shoving my cock in her pussy until she's begging me to let her come.

My dick is hard in my pants. Fuck.

"What's the schedule?" I question while getting off the ground. I reach a hand down for Larysa to grab and her fingers wrap around mine. The instant she touches me, I'm feeling like a teenage boy about to nut in my pants again.

This is fucking crazy.

Alto lightly pulls her from me and wraps her into his chest. Are they together? I'm questioning this as he is constantly trying to touch her. It makes me wonder. If they're together, he needs to be doing more to this gorgeous body. A woman who's getting dick on the regular shouldn't light up like she is.

"Larysa is on tour for the next two months and has this week off. I'm going to need someone with me at all times to watch her."

The whole week with her? I'm curious to know how that is going to go especially if they are together.

"So, I'm just going to ask. Are you two together? If so, this is going to make the situation a little difficult. You know how hard it is to protect someone when you're that close," I throw out there. I'm eager to know the truth.

Larysa clears her throat. "No!" She blurts out. "I mean, no. We're not together."

My intentions of keeping this next week professional have flown out the window at hearing she isn't with Alto. Normally I wouldn't care if a woman is taken or not. It doesn't mean fuck all to me. I'm not the marrying kind. After watching all of these marriages come to an end, I'm not interested in the institution.

There is something about this pop star in front of me that has me wanting to taste her.

Alto rubs the back of his neck, backing away from her. "Why does it matter if we are?"

I shake my head standing to my full height. "It matters because I don't need a jealous boyfriend hanging over my shoulder trying to tell me how to do my job. What are you doing this week that you're off?"

She smiles lightly. "I'm going to my house in Greece and burning sheets."

I smirk. "Sounds like you should." I pull out a card from my back pocket and slide it over to her. "Call me when you're ready to check out and I'll follow you home."

Alto is looking at how quickly Larysa takes the card out of my hand and mutters something under his breath.

I take this time to leave the room and go back to talk to Octavious. I'm thinking Alto is going to be a problem and I'm not interested in some jealous fuckery from him. It is obvious he's not protecting her the way he should be because she's still being stalked.

I'm about to the elevator when a hand grabs my shoulder. I'm instantly reaching behind me to grab my gun when Alto's voice speaks.

"Emilio, this woman means a lot to me."

"Don't ever roll up behind me like that," I mutter and turn to face him. "I get she's important to you. This is a job for me. What can I do for you?"

He smirks knowingly. "I think you want it to be something more. Don't fuck with my girl, Emilio."

I grin back at him. The threat he was trying to give me falls in the air because I don't take it. "I know you mean that as a threat, but you're the one out of your element now. You still want my help?" I ask.

Alto considers what I'm asking before answering honestly. I know he needs me. I have a way of weeding out people to finding the truth without getting caught. I don't need a clean-up crew to handle my mess, either.

"Yes, I need it."

I nod my head in agreeance. He does need me and the thing that bothers him the most, I can see how much he's in love with Larysa. "You do.

I'm one of the only people in Greece who can find this guy and bring him to our own poetic justice."

Leaving him with that thought, I go out to find Octavious. The whole way to Octavious's new office at the ski lodge, I'm thinking about that gorgeous woman. She's sexy as fuck. She's absolutely perfect.

I can see why men and women have crushes on her.

I walk into Octavious's office without knocking.

"What did you find out?"

I smirk. "I'm pretty positive her bodyguard is in love with her. He's constantly touching her."

The boss shrugs. "Yeah, not our problem. Are you still taking the job?"

It is my turn to consider my options. I want to be around this woman as much as I can for some reason. She's so sexy and I'm dying to taste her.

More than that, I felt something I haven't felt in a long time. Passion. Electric currents rolling off of her in droves.

"Yeah. I'm going to be busy with this for the next week."

He shrugs again. "Not concerned. Get the money upfront."

Chapter Four

Larysa

I'm standing in the middle of my home in Greece and I feel how much my home has been tainted. It isn't the same as it once was. My home is just walls now.

Emilio is standing behind me and taps me on the shoulder. His being here is making everything real for me. "Want to give me a tour?"

I turn to look at him while holding my jacket tighter across my body. I'm suddenly aware of how big my home is but with Emilio here, everything feels smaller. It feels tighter.

"Yeah, sure."

I walk him through the kitchen, living room, sitting room, my recording studio, my safe room off of my recording studio and then finally the bedrooms. I point to the one off of my room and open the door.

"This is your room while here," I whisper suddenly nervous. His room is way too close to my bedroom making me even more aware of how close he is to me.

He smirks. "Thanks, Larysa. Which one is yours?"

I nod to the room off to the left next to the stairs. Cautiously, I push open the door to show him the room and the way he walks in just tells me everything he wanted to look for more reasons than just my protection.

When I bought the home, I spent a lot of time decorating for it to look like my perfect home. I'm native to Greece and Greece will always be my home. I wanted the colors to be blue and white, Greek colors, along with a nice sized tank in my room.

The tank is adjacent to the fireplace nestled into the wall under the television. Inside the fish tank, I spent a lot of time choosing fish that would support serenity. The fish are colorful, calming and everything I wanted.

In the corner of my room, my closet is situated. Emilio takes the time to look at the closet, the fireplace and then back to the fish tank. He eyes me up and down with a wicked crooked grin on his full lips. I see his eyes flickering to the bed.

My insides are all over the place since it has been a long time since I've had sex. I'm overly frustrated.

"So, yeah. This is my room."

His fingers trace on the bedspread before stopping at the pillows. "Nice room."

I shrug. "I'm not here nearly enough. I'm glad I was able to find someone to look in on my fish while I'm gone." I don't know why I'm rambling but I feel as if I have to explain things to him. I feel like I have to tell him everything.

"What is your schedule for tomorrow?" Emilio asks.

"I have show practice in the morning and then a workout. I should be done around four. After, I'm going to dinner with a friend I've had forever," I let him know.

"I'll be ready to go to practice at eight. See you in the morning," he instructs before turning around.

I'm left in my room where the stalker was at. I can smell the freshly cleaned sheets, towels along with everything else that had to be cleaned. There was no way I would have been back to my room to sleep if the room hadn't been properly cleaned.

I yawn while walking over towards my bathroom. I have every intention on taking a bath with bubbles to help soothe me. I'm scared, anxious and now sexually frustrated. I need something to take the edge off.

Running the water in the bathtub, I strip out of my clothes. I flick my fingers under the water faucet to check the temperature before adding bubbles. I grab a towel off the rack and place it on top of the toilet. My nipples are pebbled while begging for attention. I'm not even going to think about the amount of arousal coursing through my body from being so close to Emilio.

I shouldn't be this attracted to him. I shouldn't be this horny to a random person but I can't help it. I want to jump on his lap, pull his pants down and ride him until we're both writhing in pleasure.

"Jesus. I'm too sexually frustrated to concentrate," I mutter to myself.

Carefully, I climb into my tub after making sure the water is just right. I'm rubbing the bubbles over my skin when one of the bottles along the edge of the tub fall to the ground.

The clambering noise is loud, echoing throughout the bathroom.

"Larysa!"

In seconds, the door to my room pushes open and Emilio is standing in front of me. "What happened?"

My tongue feels like lead in my mouth. He's only wearing tight Armani briefs. Why is this happening to me? I shouldn't be this turned on by him. I shouldn't be looking at him like I'm a hungry bitch who is starving over a random guy.

"I'm fine," I manage to say. "The bottle fell to the floor."

He's looking at me up and down while concentrating on the mounds of my tits which are flirting under the soap. I cover my boobs in hopes of maintaining some modesty but the damage had been done. He saw them.

"Fuck. Be careful next time!"

Emilio doesn't say anything else while spinning on his heels to get out of my room.

My lips open to ask him to come back.

I choose to keep my invitation to myself.

Chapter Five

Emilio

Even in my sexiest dreams, I would never have pictured her in the bathtub. She's gorgeous, sexy and her eyes were eating me up. She's so fucking sexy I couldn't even stop looking at her all vulnerable in the bathtub.

I rub the back of my neck trying to calm down my erection. Larysa is going to be the death of me and I have to figure out how to make sure I keep this as professional as possible.

I refuse to jack off like a fucking horny teenager. I refuse to whack off in the shower.

There is a light knock on the door making me shake out of my pity party. "What?" I call out through the door and swing it open.

Standing in front of me is Larysa with her hair in a pony and pajamas on. Her pajamas are not sexy but cute with the wide-legged pants and off-the-shoulder sweater. Her hair is tied in a top knot with little pieces of hair falling.

She looks amazing. I'm yearning to pull her into the room, push her against the wall and start kissing her from the top of her head until I get to her toes. Spending special attention on the part in the middle.

"Need something?" I bark out. Being this close to Larysa is dangerous for me. My dick is already begging to come out and play with her... This is just confusing me even more.

"I just, uh," she begins with her eyes tracing me up and down until she gets to the bulge in my pants. "I just wanted to apologize for earlier."

"What about earlier?" I question. I'm not letting her get off this easily. She came over here to fuck with me some more and I don't need it. I need to get my brain out of my cock and start focusing on the job.

Larysa's eyes travel up to me and scan my face until she reaches my lips. She licks her lips seductively and walks a little closer.

I take a step back. "No."

She blinks a couple of times. "No?"

I nod. "No."

"No what?"

"You're looking at me like you want to kiss me."

"I am? I didn't know I was..."

I walk away from the doorway into the main part of the room hoping to get some much-needed space. She's walking up behind me but stops before she is close enough to touch me.

"I'm not going to kiss you. I'm not the type of man that stops at kissing. I'm the type of man that stops with my dick buried in your tight pussy until you beg me to stop."

Her eyes widen.

"Too dirty?" I taunt.

"I…"

Smirking at her, I point towards the door. "If that is too much for you, I'm not the one for you. I'm not interested in being your walk on the wild side. I'm not interested in being a play toy. Me fucking you into the mattress isn't going to keep you safe. Good night."

She looks frustrated and surprised at my bluntness. "I'm sorry," she mutters.

I shrug. "Peaches, I'm not the kind of guy you put in your Barbie Dreamhouse. I need to get some sleep."

Chapter Six

Larysa

Did that really just happen? I don't know what I was expecting by coming over to his room this late at night in my pajamas. I don't know if I was expecting him to make love to me all night or if I just wanted to see him again.

I knew that stupid reasoning for wanting to apologize wasn't going to be enough right now. Emilio isn't stupid and he's not the kind of guy who would fall for those tricks.

I take my defeated ass back to my room, crawl into the bed but then remember what happened in here. My bedroom has been tainted. I have no want to stay here anymore.

I grab a pillow off the bed then walk out of my room. I'm in the middle of the hallway when Emilio's door cracks open. He's staring at me with his eyes wide. "What are you doing?"

I shrug. "I can't sleep in there. Don't worry. I'm not running away," I mumble under my breath. He has a way of making me feel stupid and I don't like it.

His hand reaches out of the door to grab me by my elbow. "You move rooms, you tell me. Until your stalker is caught, every move you make has to be approved by me. Do you get me?"

I nod. "I just can't sleep in there," I whisper.

"What do you want to do?"

"Watch a movie."

We're still standing in the middle of the hallway having this conversation. It is in this moment I realize Emilio isn't who I thought he was. Sure, he's a rough man but I think he actually cares about me.

Unless I'm crazy.

"I have a movie theater downstairs with recliners. Do you want to watch a movie with me?" I ask him.

Emilio considers my suggestion. "Give me two minutes," he mutters then runs back into his room.

I'm standing there stupidly waiting for him to come back. From the top of my stairs, you can see the road from the windows. I'm looking outside trying to see if there is anything out of the ordinary. I don't see anything but that doesn't mean anything.

Suddenly, off in the distance, I could have sworn I saw a flash go off. I scream making Emilio run out of his room with his arms wrapping around my waist. He pulls me to the ground with his gorgeous body on top of mine.

I'm very aware of his body in this position.

"What happened?"

"I saw a flash from the window."

Emilio pops up off me making me miss his weight automatically. I like feeling him on top of me. He's looking out the window with his sweatpants bottoms on and I can still see his Armani waistband to his underwear.

"I don't see anyone outside. Let's get down to your theater room and tomorrow I will check it out when Alto is back."

I don't reply because there really isn't anything for me to say. He has everything figured out without my help. I must admit- it is very sexy.

Leading him down the stairs, I check to make sure the alarm to the house is still secured. After seeing that it is, I continue to lead him to the back of the house where my theater is.

One of the things I love to do is watch movies and not worry about everyone else in the theater. Plus, I like to watch movies in pitch black with a blanket on.

Once in the room, I flick on a couple of lights while grabbing the remote to the television. I pull up all of the movies I have stored and begin to ask Emilio which genres he likes.

"I like anything really. Just no chick flicks."

I smirk. "I thought you would love watching Brokeback Mountain," I retort snidely.

I don't fully hear his response but it sounded like he threatened to spank me.

We choose a movie and I take the seat next to Emilio. We're sitting in a loveseat with a recliner attached to it. I'm snuggled in my blanket with my body slightly curled into Emilio's side. A couple of times throughout the movie, he places his hand on my leg or thigh.

The man is killing me.

By the time we got to the second movie, I definitely felt as if I was getting tired. I close my eyes for just a few moments.

 I don't wake up until I feel someone moving next to me.

Only when I open my eyes do I see what I did. I managed to fall asleep on Emilio's shoulder who is now trying to get comfortable with me sleeping on him. The room is dark and luckily he doesn't know I'm awake.

His arm slips around my shoulders and he's cradling me to his chest as if I'm precious to him.

Chapter Seven

Emilio

I'm startled awake from one of the best nights sleep I have had in a long time. I reach out around me to get a better sense of where I'm at.

The bed I'm on is stretched out with a slight uphill to the back of the bed. I then look down to see a splash of hair stretched out over my arm, chest and my neck. I'm looking down at her and then I remember what happened.

We fell asleep watching a movie together and ended up cuddling in front of the movie screen.

How long has it been since I have cuddled with a woman? How long has it been since I actually slept with a woman? I can't remember the last time any of those happened.

It's a strange feeling being this close to Larysa and it is a strange feeling knowing how much I like it.

As soon as I started to become more affiliated with the Andinos, my life changed dramatically. I didn't sleep with a lot of women even though they all liked the prestige of my affiliation. I didn't want to drag a woman into the life making all of our relationships together just sexual.

I fight the urge to gather her hair together and pulling her to my mouth. I can't even begin to process what that means for me. I have lived a hard life and being this close to this woman is doing weird things to me.

Larysa slowly starts to wake up and I pull myself away from her to not startle her. I don't need her thinking I'm trying to get something from her. She might be a pop star but I have a lot more money than she has and more power throughout the world just by me being a soldier for the Andinos.

"Good morning," she whispers all sleepily.

I fight the urge yet again to kiss her.

With more strength and resistance than I thought I had, I untangle her from me as much as I can. I need to put some distance between us.

"What time is rehearsal?"

She groggily pulls her phone out of her pocket to check the time. "Now. Shit."

I smirk slightly. "Are your rehearsals here or are they someplace else?"

"What the fuck is going on here?" Alto demands snidely. I can see how annoyed he is that I'm here and he isn't. I can also see how jealous he is.

I wonder how long he's wanted to fuck Larysa. The look on his face tells me everything. I want to fuck with him some to get him going, but I decide against it.

"I came down here to see why you weren't at rehearsals, but I guess I see why," Alto retorts.

Larysa is quick to her defense. "You're my bodyguard and not my father," she replies with venom dripping from her words. "Anyways, I'm on my way to rehearsal now."

With that, she climbs out of the seat and begins to walk herself out of the theater room. The minute the door shuts behind her, Alto is trying to attack me. Bad move, mother fucker.

"How dare you take advantage of her!"

I have to chuckle at that insinuation. Getting out of the seat, I'm standing toe to toe with Alto. "I don't owe you shit. You need to get out of my face before I do something about it. I'm not the type of person you fuck with."

"We won't be needing you for the rehearsal today," he clips.

"You hired me. She's paying me. You're not the boss here. Get out of my way so I can get dressed."

I don't let him say anything more as I'm walking out of the room. I'm up in my room in a minute to shower quickly and get dressed when my phone rings from the bedside table.

"Hello?" I answer.

"Any closer to finding out anything?" Miklos demands.

Miklos is a scary bastard who can find anything on anyone online. Even though he isn't Greek by birth, he's been an excellent addition to the Andinos.

"No, but I do have a mission for you."

He chuckles. "I wonder what it's like to be that close to the pop star. Did you know she's sold a shit ton of albums and all that bull shit?"

"Are we going to drive around with the top down now after getting expensive iced coffees?"

"Fiesty! What do you want?"

"I need all the info you can get on Alto. He's Larysa's bodyguard."

I hear him tapping at the keyboard before clearing his throat. "You sure about this?"

"Do it."

"Octavious wants you to call him. He needs to send you out on a job real quick."

Smirking, I hang up the phone. Octavious rattles off the information needed to do the job. In fifteen minutes, I'm out the door and ready to get this shit done.

Harry Sidarikus was a trusted soldier to the Andinos for more than fifteen years until he got caught murdering a family outside of Mount Olympus. He killed the two parents and the two children in broad daylight because of reasons only he knows.

Long story short, Harry killed this family in front of an off-duty cop who brought him and demanded he ratted. Harry couldn't wait to get out of custody and ratted way too quickly. The dumb mother fucker then tried to steal money from us. Little did Harry know, the safe room has video recordings at all times.

I pull into his safe house with my gun cocked and ready to go. I don't need to play games with him since he knows what is about to happen. Like the safe house is going to keep him safe from me. It is almost insulting how easy they made this.

I knock on the door and give Harry the secret code word to get him to answer the door. Once Harry sees me, he gets down to his knees to start begging.

"I'm so sorry, Emilio! I'm so fucking sorry! They were going to lock me up for life. I can't do life," he begins to beg.

The once most trusted soldier for the Andinos has been reduced to nothing more than a sniveling man. He's a piece of shit who doesn't deserve to live anymore.

"I don't care about your reasonings. You ratted and then tried to steal money? How stupid can you be?"

My gun is aimed at his head. The fucker is still begging but none of that matters anymore. I squeeze the trigger and watch him drop quickly to the ground.

I place my gun in the back of my pants then drag him towards the bathroom. After mixing the cocktail that melts a body, I place Harry into the bathtub then douse him with the solution.

It happens quickly.

Good.

I need to get back to Larysa.

"It's done," I say to Octavious on the phone.

"No problems?"

"None. I gotta go back to my job now."

I'm pulling into Larysa's driveway as she's walking people out of her home. She doesn't see me but I see and hear her.

"He's so hot. I don't know…"

"What do you mean? You have a thing for your new bodyguard?"

"You would, too, if you met him!"

"I don't know. I don't have a thing for the help."

"He might be my bodyguard but he's sexy!"

"I know he's sexy! You think my lady parts don't know that? I'm way too turned on," Larysa whines.

Clearing my throat, I slam the door shut on my car. The five ladies surrounding Larysa spin on their heels and look me up and down.

"Holy shit!"

"Ladies, you're all looking beautiful," I reply with a wicked smile on my face. My eyes eat Larysa up. "Especially good morning to you, beautiful," I tell her with a wink.

Chapter Eight

Larysa

"What was it like to have that sexy man sleeping next to you?" Kai gushes as she puts on her shoes after rehearsal.

Kai has been with me for many years and has seen the world with me. I love how out there she is along with how adventurous she is. The woman is all of five feet and less than a hundred pounds but is full of attitude.

"Uh, I don't know. I was asleep."

She smirks a knowing smile. "He walked in on you while you were in the tub?"

I roll my eyes. "I shouldn't have told you that," I quip while stretching.

The rehearsal was longer because I needed to keep myself occupied from the thoughts of the sexy man staying in my house. The truth is, I don't know anything about him. I also don't know if he is remotely interested in me.

My body burns from the workout but it's my brain and heart that can still go a couple of more hours. I'm hoping I'm able to work out the frustrations of my lack of sexual activity today. It hasn't helped, but I'm hoping it does.

I'm mortified. Utterly and completely mortified. I never thought he would come back this early after he took off so quickly without saying anything to me.

He heard me say how sexually frustrated I was? Jesus. Can the floor eat me up? Please. For the love of all that is holy. Please swallow me whole!

The truth is, I have been flying high all day thinking about what it was like being with Emilio last night. I'm going to be honest with myself and admit it was one of the best nights I have slept in a long time.

"Holy shit," every girl whispers as they surround Emilio.

Emilio eats it up with a smile. "Ladies, what do I owe this pleasure of seeing such beautiful women this early?"

Kai is in slut heaven. "If you don't want him, I will take him," she whispers loudly towards me.

I want to punch her in the face. How dare she call me out like that!

"All right, everyone! I need to shower!" I yell trying to get the three girls who are circling around Emilio to leave. My jealousy is something I never expected.

They all turn to leave while smiling at Emilio. Emilio's eyes look the ladies up and down before winking at me.

This is only day two. We have five more days until I leave Greece to go back on tour. I don't know how I'm going to be able to handle all of this. I especially don't know how I can keep my hands to myself.

The girls turn to leave and I'm waving at them as they climb into their cars. "See you tomorrow!" I call out before turning around to walk into the house.

Once I turn, I feel hands on hips and the warmth of a sexy alpha male. My mind tells me to push him away and my heart tells me to pull him closer. My girly parts tell me to strip out of my clothes and climb him like a tree.

However, the night before I was naked in a bathtub and he didn't care at all. He didn't care that I was naked and all he had to do was reach between my legs to feel me.

I shake off those unwarranted thoughts. I don't need to think that way when my breathing is picking up and I'm wanting to mold myself to him.

"I can see all those dirty thoughts in your head, Larysa. I can see how much they turn you on. I can see also how much you want me. When you're ready to admit it, I'll let you have a taste for what it is like to have a bad boy."

His words do funny things to me. I can't help it. I can't help but want him in every way. The worst part is, I know he's dangerous but I don't know how dangerous he is.

"Why?" I mutter. I'm not sure why I'm asking him that and I'm not sure what the answer is I'm wanting to get. I do know I'm wanting something from him I don't know how to ask.

He gets closer to me so I can smell his musk and his natural scent. He smells amazingly intoxicating. Something I never knew I would like. Something I would never think to want.

I haven't been with someone in a long time because I'm not sure if they are interested in me or my status of being a pop star. I have no idea.

What I do know is I'm willing to put down my walls and open my legs to him. Even for the day.

"Princess, you're wanting to taste what it is like to be with the bad boy. I'm the bad boy who you're going to get lost into. I need you to make sure you understand that before you jump on."

With that, he leaves me a wanton mess.

Chapter Nine

Emilio

I'm watching tapes of her concerts in the watch room as she's in the kitchen making something to eat. I'm anxious to see what I can see when all of a sudden there is a crash in the kitchen.

I see lightning and the glass shattering along the outside of the kitchen.

Pushing out of my seat, I run towards the kitchen to see Larysa hunched over with her hands on her ears. Larysa is shaking from the explosion but it's the look of utter horror that keeps me from examining what is going on.

I'm rushing over to her and drop to my knees to pull her into me. She is trembling from being afraid.

She is wrapping her arms around me to hold me tighter to her. I love the feeling of her being wrapped in my arms.

"Why is this happening to me? What did I do? I don't understand?"

"Baby, you didn't do anything. Sometimes this shit happens," I reply.

I'm rubbing my hands down her back with a little detour to around her round hips. She smells like lavender and vanilla all at once. Her lips lightly brush against mine and I lose it.

I'm grabbing her by the waist pulling her on top of me in the middle of the kitchen. Her little shorts provide her no protection from the raspiness of my jeans.

"You sure about this?" I ask one time. "I'm not going to be able to stop," I admit.

She nods. "Please make me feel."

I push up against her warm pussy for her to feel the outline of my dick. She mewls in the back of her throat. I roll over so she's under me and I'm on top. She looks amazing with her hair all scattered along with the tile of the floor.

My lips trail from hers, to her throat, collarbone and then to the mounds of her tits. I'm sucking on her delicious nipples through her thin tank top making them pebble under my tongue. She thrusting her body against mine trying to get as much friction as she can to get off.

"Shit! Please!" Larysa begs.

My hands travel up and down her body until I'm reaching the center where she is aching for me the most. She lets out a large cry as I finger her through her little shorts.

She's hot and tight and ready to explode under me.

My lips trail down her once more until I'm reaching the waistband of her shorts. I yank them down off her until I see her beautiful pussy begging for me.

I know I'm about to come in my pants like a little asshole who's never had pussy before. She's fucking gorgeous.

"Get on your hands and knees," I demand.

She's quick to do as I ask. I dive in behind with my tongue spearing her from behind. She writhes under my touch, clearly enjoying it. My tongue tickles her clit, pistons inside of her sweet hole over and over until she's screaming loudly.

"I'm going to come! I'm going to come!"

I pick up my pace to drive her even crazier. When I feel her begin to squirm more, I stop what I'm doing and insert two fingers inside of her and one in her forbidden back entrance. She yelps with the intrusion then fucks my fingers.

This woman was made for sex.

"You going to come?" I taunt.

"Yes! Please! Let me come."

I fuck her harder with my fingers and when she's moaning louder than before, I stop what I'm doing.

I shove my pants down and ram inside of her. I'm fucking her harder with my dick as my balls slap against her clit.

"I need… I need it!" Larysa begs.

Again, I stick my finger in her ass just to feel her tighten around me. She's going to become my own personal brand of heroin.

"Fuck!" I shout as she squeezes me and makes me lose control. I piston my hips harder, faster inside of her tight hole.

I can't stop myself from coming inside of her when she shakes around me and yells out her orgasm. I'm thrusting in and out of her as my own orgasm comes crashing through me.

Larysa collapses underneath me clearly spent. My dick is still hard inside of her and I roll her over to continue. I'm not done yet.

I'm on top of her with my finger still lodged up in her back entrance. She's whining and bucking against me to continue once more.

"Free your tits," I demand. She instantly does what I ask.

My lips and teeth grab onto each of her nipples as I drive deeper and deeper inside of her. She's coming again.

"Sweet fucking shit," I murmur against her tit. "You're going to kill me," I tell her as I empty myself inside of her again.

Her legs are shaking around me and she is screaming out her orgasm yet again. This woman is so responsive.

Chapter Ten

Larysa

No one has ever made me come that hard in my life before. I have no idea how he could make me lose control like that but I loved it.

I'm in the shower with the side shower jets massaging my overworked muscles I haven't used in a long time. I don't know what this means and if it means anything to him, but I enjoyed it.

I don't know if this means he likes me or if he wanted to drive me crazy with lust but mission accomplished. I do like him and he drove me insane with want.

I'm about ready to get out when my shower door swings open to show me a sexy man who made me come too many times in one sexual experience standing in front of me. Naked.

He lets himself in my shower and begins to hose off the sweat with the hot water. I see he's hard again making me remember I didn't return the favor of servicing him with my mouth.

I get down to my knees and grip the base of his dick and cup his balls with my hands. He grunts slightly while placing his hands on the back shower wall.

"Swallow me whole," he mutters through gritted teeth.

I breathe deeply then take him as deep as I can into the back of my throat. My hand meets my thrust over and over as I swallow him whole. Emilio's grunting is enough for me to feel empowered.

I take turns between squeezing his balls and jacking him off with my hand to meet the rhythm of my mouth. I use my teeth to tease him a little making him drop his hands down to my hair to pull me up.

"Wrap your legs around my waist," he mutters.

I'm quick to follow him and allow him to help me do what he's asking me to do. The minute I'm wrapped around him again, he's plowing into me.

My pussy has stretched to full capacity to allow him inside.

"You feel so fucking good," he whispers against my ear.

My body spasms for what feels like the one hundredth time today around him. "I... I love feeling you inside of me," I moan. "Fuck me harder."

He does what I ask him to do. The tiles are warm behind me allowing me to slip on them to meet his dick even more.

I'm shouting out my orgasm yet again in the bathroom as it echoes throughout the whole bathroom.

He follows behind me and yells out.

"I'm not gonna lie, baby. Your pussy is addictive as fuck."

I should be upset over how crass he is. However, it makes me feel good. It makes me feel as if he likes me just as much as I like him.

"I hope you know what this means," he asks before kissing me soundly on the lips.

"Huh?" I ask. My brain is drowning in sexiness and the thought of answering him any other way isn't going to happen.

He chuckles with his dick still inside of me. I'm too far spent to have this conversation with him.

"This means you're mine. Your mine to do what I want with and your mine to possess."

The thought of him claiming me shouldn't make me this giddy but it does. I love the thought of him wanting me as much as I want him. I love the thought of him being so possessive over me he wants to claim me.

"Let's get dressed and then get some dinner," he orders.

Emilio helps me off of him with his dick still inside of me. The new positions as the stretching between my legs make me moan all over again.

He winks. "Later. I gotta feed you."

*

"Something smells good," I praise as I walk into the kitchen.

I'm dressed in a sundress with the back cut out and a pair of flip flops. My hair swishes around my back effectively tickling me.

I have seen Emilio naked, I have seen him in the throes of passion but seeing him in loose-fitting jeans is something I never thought was sexy. He turns to look at me with his chest bare and a small splattering of hair on it. He doesn't have any tattoos but his almost-six pack is still sexy.

"I hope you're hungry," he replies with a wink.

"Starving…" I'm not lying either. I haven't had sex in a long time and I'm feeling the exertion of the workout.

Emilio is walking around my kitchen like he owns it. I have lived here for quite a while and have never used the kitchen like he has right now. In fact, I don't know how old any of those spices are in the cabinets nor did I know I had spices. My idea of eating dinner is usually ordering something through takeout.

"Well, I guess this is one thing I learned about you," I inform him with a smile. "I didn't know you knew how to cook."

He's been living with me for a short amount of time and there is no way for me to learn anything of substance about him. I do know he's amazing in bed… and the shower…

"My mother is from Italy and my father is a pure Greek through and through. I learned how to cook at a young age. My father always told me the way a man cooks is how he makes love. I took that as he meant it."

My body is heating just thinking about making love to him again. "Well, you do that very well," I admit. "What else?"

He's bringing over the two plates with a dirty yet promising smile on his face. "What do you want to know?"

"What do you do for a living?"

Chapter Eleven

Emilio

I'm dressed and down in the kitchen before she even makes it down. I decided to make her something simple and not too complicated as I don't know what she likes to eat. She might be one of those people who eat very healthily or might be one of those people who only eat junk.

I like a woman who can eat a burger and drink a milkshake myself. I hate when women are too afraid to eat something good because they are embarrassed.

She looks beautiful when she entered the kitchen and she smiles at me as she accepts the plate of food I made her. It feels so normal to be like this with her. I don't know why but I like it.

In fact, I think I can get used to this fucking domesticated bliss.

"What do you do for a living?" Larysa asks.

"Uh…"

She smiles with her pearly whites flashing in the light. "I just want to know. I'm not going to stalk you."

I could tell her the truth. I could tell her right now that I'm in the mafia or I could make something up. I don't know which one would be better.

"I'm in security," I reply. I won't elaborate because I don't want to ruin the evening. The last thing I want to discuss is that I'm in the mafia and am a paid-to-hire-hitman.

She seems okay with that answer and moves on. Throughout our dinner, she tells me about touring, about her family, friends and how she got involved in being a pop star. She's incredible. I've kept the information about me very slim for the obvious reasons.

With our dinner being finished, I'm about to make my move to put Larysa on the counter to fuck her again when the doorbell rings.

"Who's that?" I ask her in case she has someone else coming to the home I don't know about.

She instantly tenses behind me and I can see the color draining from her face. Whoever is at the door has wrecked the entire evening.

"Stay here," I mutter and leave the kitchen. I'm reaching behind me to grab my gun with it aimed at the door. "Who is it?"

I hear the familiar voice of Miklos. "Answer the door, Emilio. It's me."

I swing open the door and give him a glaring look. "What are you doing here?"

"You wouldn't answer your phone and you have to see this."

He's walking through the house until he gets to the living room. Miklos makes himself at home with his computer turned on ready for me to see why he's invading our space. The Hungarian gives me a look that tells me I'm not going to like this.

Larysa is walking up behind me with her eyes eating up the whole scene. "Who is this?"

"I'm Miklos. I'm a-"

"A friend of mine," I finish. I don't want him to say he's an associate or anything mafia-related for the obvious reasons.

One of the camera feeds pop up on Miklos's computer and he spins it around for me to take a look. "This isn't one the security set up. This is the one someone else set up."

"Who?" Larysa demands.

I can see the camera feed on the shower where I had her pinned up against the wall. I know exactly who it could be. It has to be Alto.

"How long have you been with Alto?" I demand.

She shakes her head. "It can't be him. I've been with him forever!"

I hold her close to me. "Baby, it has to be Alto. He's the only one who would have cameras in your room and bathroom. Think about it."

Larysa's tears are soaking my shirt. "It can't be."

Miklos coughs and clears his throat to get us to look back at his computer. Sure enough, he's pulled up the feed of us fucking in the shower.

"I'm going to kill him," I mutter to myself.

"He can't be the one stalking me! Why would he do that?" Larysa whines. "I don't understand."

I'm walking towards the door with Miklos with me. Miklos stops and looks back at Larysa before getting my attention.

"We'll call one of the guys to sit with her," he says.

"Where are you going?" Larysa demands.

"I'm going hunting."

Chapter Twelve

Larysa

The thought of my bodyguard being my stalker is something I would have never assumed. Watching them walk out of my house, I feel something I didn't expect to feel.

I feel a sense of longing for Emilio. Two days of knowing him and a handful of orgasms has me missing a man I know nothing about.

There's a knock on the door about fifteen minutes after the guys left. I run over to the door to open it since I knew the guys sent someone else over to sit with me.

"Larysa."

My mouth drops and I start to back away from him. The man who has kept me safe all of this time is the man who has been stalking me. It doesn't make any sense. There has to be a reason for this to be happening to me. There has to be a simple and logical reason for this.

"Why?" I ask him while walking back towards thc living room.

He's on me quickly. He has me pressed up against the wall with his whole body weight keeping me still. "I have loved you since the moment I met you and you could have loved me. You could have been with me this whole time and yet you didn't see me. I don't understand why!"

His lips are on mine and he's kissing me ferociously. This is something I would have never assumed him to do.

I can't believe it. I'm stock still as his lips move down my throat and his hands are feeling up my body quickly. It happens so suddenly. His fingers are delving inside of my underwear when I feel the scream bubbling up inside of me.

"Stop! Please stop," I beg.

He doesn't stop. In fact, he growls at me. "You weren't asking that lowlife to stop. You know he's in the mafia? You know he's killed people before."

My mind is racing with the information he's telling me. It couldn't be true. I would know if he was in the mafia, wouldn't I? What do people in the mafia look like?

"You dirty little whore. I can't believe you let him touch you. I waited for you to love me. I thought this would make you run into my arms. I can't believe you," he rambles on.

I'm shaking with everything he's telling me. I can't believe it. "No," I mutter.

"Think about it, Larysa. I loved you so much I wanted you all to myself. I loved you through everything and all you had to do was love me, too. That's it," he continues.

"I don't want you," I manage to squeak out.

His hand leaves my sex and suddenly they are wrapped around my neck. He's squeezing me to the point where I'm losing vision. "You dirty little whore," he implores once more.

I'm wheezing as the black spots in my vision begin to take over even more.

Suddenly, he's off of me and I can breathe again.

Chapter Thirteen

Emilio

Something inside of me began to consider the options and the opportunity Alto would have if we left and I knew where he would be heading. It wouldn't have taken a genius to figure it out.

"We have to turn around," I order. "I need to be with her."

Miklos doesn't reply and turns the vehicle around. We make it back up the driveway just as I see the light flickering in her home. There is someone who keeps walking through the light area.

"What the fuck?" I demand.

Miklos throws the car into park and we are both running up to the main door. I kick it open since it is locked and see Alto against Larysa. He's trying to kill her with his bare hands.

"You mother fucker!" I yell at him and yank him off of her. He falls to the ground with a thud.

"I told that dirty little slut all about you."

I kick him in the gut. "Did that help you get her to fall to her knees for you? She doesn't want you!"

"You think she wants you? You think she wants a mobster who is nothing? She doesn't want you."

He told her I was in the mob? This guy is slick.

"Brother, I got this," Miklos informs me from behind. "You need to be with Larysa."

I look back at my girl who is on the floor with her hand over her throat and her eyes are wide. She looks scared out of her mind.

I don't wait another second. I grab my gun and fire it at Alto's head.

Miklos is quick to pull him out of the room while I rush over to Larysa. She's screaming but grabs onto me to hold me tightly against her.

"It's okay, baby. Nothing is going to happen to you again," I hush her.

She's grappling with my shirt to hold me to her and then she lets out the most god-awful cry. "This couldn't be true. This couldn't be happening to me!"

"Baby, it's over with. You're safe!"

"You killed a man in front of me," she retorts with malice. "You legit just killed my bodyguard in front of me."

I'm trying to shake her shoulders to get her to look at me in the eyes. When she finally does, she calms slightly. "He would have done this for years if I didn't kill him. He would have stalked you for years. Baby, you didn't do anything wrong."

She nods slightly. "I, I don't know what to say."

I half-smirk at her. "Larysa, there is nothing you can say. I need you to go upstairs and shut the door so I can take care of Alto's body. Can you do that?"

Larysa is crying heavier than before. "He's dead?"

I want to laugh at her, but I don't. She's struggling with everything and I kiss her lightly on the lips.

"What happens now?"

"We get to know each other and see where this goes," I reply.

Larysa looks back at Alto and then at me. "Thank you for saving me."

Epilogue

Larysa

News circulated really quickly about my engagement to Emilio. He's been with me to a majority of my shows and finally asked me to marry him two nights ago in New York. In the middle of the event space, he dropped down on one knee to give me the most beautiful ring in the world.

Splashed across all of the tabloids is our picture with some sort of title about *Pop Princess to Marry Mobster!*

I'm looking down at my ring with Emilio wrapped around me. We have been having some amazing sex and I can't wait until he wakes up for us to continue.

The mattress in the hotel room we are staying in broke last night when he fucked me so hard it cracked. I'm giggling at the thought of him doing it to me again.

"What's so funny, baby?" Emilio asks sleepily.

"I guess you really did fuck me into the mattress."

He chuckles. "Better be careful. I'll do it again."

"I'm going to hold you to that."

The End.

I hope you enjoyed Larysa and Emilio's fast-burn romance! While these stories are aimed to be shorter for you to get as much action and sexiness quickly, please check out my other books that are out.

I love you all,

Eden

www.ingramcontent.com/pod-product-compliance
Lightning Source LLC
Chambersburg PA
CBHW071951120726

48001CB00005B/2130